A lady from El Salvador once described her loving memories of the *nacimiento* (nativity scene) she used to set up around Christmas. Early on, she would plant corn seeds and use the seedlings as greenery against a painted Salvadoran countryside. She would create slopes and hills using dyed sawdust that she got from her carpenter husband. Using mirrors for water and the smallest clay figurines from the region of Ilobasco, she would create a whole village. As the holiday approached, her three kings slowly approached the manger. And the child was added on Christmas Eve when He was "born."

Las Navidades

Popular Christmas Songs from Latin America

Selected and illustrated by Lulu Delacre

English lyrics by Elena Paz
Musical arrangements by Ana-María Rosado

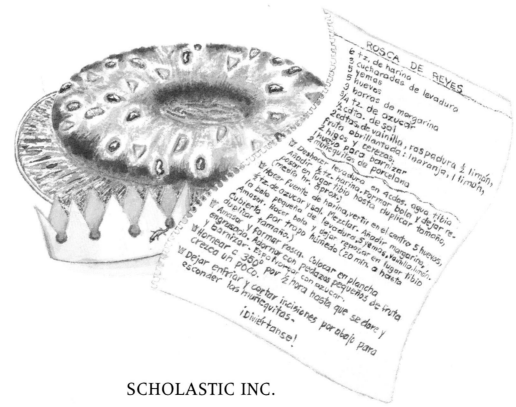

ROSCA DE REYES
6 tz. de harina
3 cucharadas de levadura
5 yemas
3 huevos
3 barras de margarina
3/4 tz. de azúcar
1/2 cdta. de sal
2cdtas. de vainilla, raspadura 1/2 limón,
fruta abrillantada: 1naranja, 1 limón,
2 higos y cerezas.
1 huevo para barnizar
2 muñequitas de porcelana

☙ Deshacer levadura en 4cdas. agua tibia
Añadir 1/2 tz. harina. Formar bola y dejar reposar en lugar tibio hasta duplicar tamaño.
(media hr. aprox.)
☙ Hacer fuente de harina, vertir en el centro 5 huevos,
3 tz. de azúcar y sal. Mezclar. Añadir margarina,
la bola pequeña de levadura, 5 yemas, vainilla, limón.
Amasar. Hacer bola y dejar reposar en lugar tibio
cubierto por trapo húmedo (20 min. a hasta
duplicar tamaño.)
☙ Amasar y formar rosca. Colocar en plancha
engrasada. Adornar con pedazos pequeños de fruta
y barnizar. Espolvorear con azúcar.
☙ Hornear a 350° por 1/2 hora hasta que se dore y
crezca un poco.
☙ Dejar enfriar y cortar incisiones por abajo para
esconder las muñequitas.
¡Diviértanse!

SCHOLASTIC INC.

New York   Toronto   London   Auckland   Sydney

Para Ethel, con inmensa gratitud.

For Dianne, Barbara, and Dilys—for believing.

A LUCAS ● EVANS BOOK

ISBN 0-590-43549-3

12 11 10 9 8 7 6 5 4 3 2   1 2 3 4 5 6/9

Printed in the U.S.A.   08

Contenidos / Contents

Las Navidades

Por fin llegaron
las Navidades
las fiestas reales
de nuestro lar.
Fiesta de todos
nuestros anhelos,
nuestros desvelos,
y nuestro afán.

PUERTO RICO

Las Navidades comienzan con la preparación de platos típicos. He aquí puertorriqueñas preparando "pasteles." Los pasteles se forman con una masa de plátano rallado que se rellena de un guiso de res, cerdo, pasas, cebolla y aceitunas. Se envuelvan en la hoja del plátano, y se cocinan en agua hirviendo. En México, Panamá y El Salvador se prepara una versión diferente a la que llaman "tamales." En Venezuela se conocen por "hallacas" y en Nicaragua por "nacatamales."

The Christmas season always begins with the preparation of food. Here, Puerto Rican women are making *pasteles*, a holiday dish consisting of a plantain paste stuffed with beef, pork, raisins, onions, and olives, and neatly wrapped in a plantain leaf. Mexico, Panama, and El Salvador have a very similar dish called *tamales*. Venezuelans call them *hallacas*; Nicaraguans *nacatamales*.

The Christmas Season

It's finally here!
The Christmas season,
In regal splendor,
Has blessed our home.
This wonderous fiesta,
So deeply yearned for,
Our nights are sleepless,
With great desire.

cruz de malta

jengibre

morivivi

trinitaria

amapola

Hermoso bouquet

Hermoso bouquet
aquí te traemos;
bellísimas flores
del jardín riqueño.

De todas las flores
yo te traigo una rama;
recíbelo bien
que ésta es tu aguinaldo.

PUERTO RICO

Dicen que en Puerto Rico, los cañaverales parecen estar cubiertos por un manto de nieve durante diciembre. La caña de azúcar está en flor; su flor, la guajana, es tan blanca como la nieve. La guajana y la flor de Pascua aparecen para las Navidades. Aquí hay otras flores que adornan la isla durante el resto del año.

Beautiful Bouquet

Beautiful bouquet
We have come to bring you
These bewitching flowers
From the lushest garden.

One of every flower
Joins this brilliant gathering
Please accept with love
My humble Christmas present.

It is said that in December, the sugarcane fields in Puerto Rico look as though they are dusted with light snow. For then, the cane's flower, *guajana*, is in full bloom. The *guajana* and the *flor de pascuas* (poinsettia), both pictured on the cover, bloom only at Christmas. Shown here are some of the other flowers that grow year 'round on the island.

canaria

isabel II

flamboyán

Abreme la puerta

Abreme la puerta
que estoy en la calle,
y dirá la gente
que esto es un desaire.

En esta ventana
pongo yo una rosa
para que la tomen
marido y esposa.

En esta ventana
veo un bulto tapado,
no sé si será
un lechón asado.

SANTO DOMINGO

Una de las tradiciones navideñas que se celebra en Santo Domingo, Puerto Rico y Venezuela entre otros países es la "trulla" o "asalto." Un grupo de amigos se reúne para llevar una serenata a otro amigo. Afuera de la casa se quedan cantando hasta que el anfitrión les abre y obsequia con comida y bebida. Es usual que los anfitriones se unan al grupo para continuar los asaltos de casa en casa.

Open the Door

Open up the door, friends
In the street I'm waiting
People will start talking
Please do not ignore me.

At this very window
Roses I shall leave you
Hope they will be taken
By you, sire and lady.

Peeking through your window
See that mound so hidden —
Can it be? I hope —
A luscious suckling piglet!

One Christmas tradition celebrated in Santo Domingo, Puerto Rico, and Venezuela, among other countries, is called *trulla* or *asalto*. Here, a group of friends gather to serenade outside another friend's house. The host opens the door and rewards carolers with food and drink. Usually, the host joins the party to go on to the next house, etc.

Anunciación

La Virgen María
se halló embarazada
y un ángel le dijo
que no se apurara;
que se consolara
con mirarlo a El,
que habría de nacer
de su propio seno
un Dios verdadero
entre mula y buey.

PUERTO RICO

The Annunciation

The Virgin María
Found herself with child.
And an angel told her
She was not to fear.
She will be contented
When she sees His sweet face.
From deep within her
A baby will be born.
Born will be a true God
Between mule and ox.

El santero es uno de los artesanos más antiguos y reconocidos en Puerto Rico. Hace tallas en madera para representar santos y otras figuras religiosas. Las pinta, las firma y las vende como adornos o para formar parte de un nacimiento navideño.

The *santero* is one of the well-established traditional artisans in Puerto Rico. He is a woodcarver of saints and other nativity figurines. After the figures are hand carved, they are painted, signed, and sold for decoration, or most important, for the nativity scenes always so present around Christmas in Latin America.

Alegría, alegría, alegría

Hacia Belén se encamina
María con su amante esposo,
llevando en su compañía
a todo un Dios poderoso.

Alegría, alegría, alegría;
alegría, alegría y placer,
que la Virgen
va de paso
con su esposo
hacia Belén.

En Puerto Rico, al igual que en otros países de Hispanoamérica, el gran festejo ocurre en Nochebuena. Luego de la misa del gallo a medianoche, los familiares se reúnen en el hogar para el festín. Como la celebración se extiende hasta la madrugada, el día de Navidad es más bien tranquilo y recogido. (Arriba está ilustrada la iglesia de Vega Alta en Puerto Rico.)

PUERTO RICO

Oh, Rejoice, Oh, Rejoice, Oh, Rejoice!

To Bethlehem, they are going
Ah! María and José.
Almighty God, traveling with them,
He will keep them company.

Oh rejoice, Oh rejoice, Oh rejoice!
Oh rejoice, Oh rejoice, and be gay!
For approaching Bethlehem
Are María and José.

In Puerto Rico, as in many other Hispanic countries, the big Christmas celebration is on Christmas Eve. After attending *misa del gallo*, (midnight mass), people gather for a feast in their homes. Because this celebration goes on so late, Christmas day is usually calm and quiet. (Pictured above is the Village Church of Vega Alta in Puerto Rico.)

La rama

Desde Veracruz venimos andando
y al niño Jesús andamos buscando.

En un jacalito de cal y de arena
nació Jesucristo en la Nochebuena.

Salgan para afuera, verán qué primores,
verán a la rama cubierta de flores.

Naranjas y limas, limas y limones:
más chula es la Virgen que todas las flores.

MEXICO

Según cuenta la tradición navideña que se origina en Veracruz, México, los niños, y a veces los adultos, forman una procesión y llevan una rama de árbol adornada con luces, flores y pedazos de papel de colores. Van de casa en casa, van cantando, pidiendo aguinaldo. Se les dan golosinas y a veces hasta monedas.

The Flowering Branch

From Veracruz we have all come walking,
And for Baby Jesus, we have all been looking.

In a little hut made of sand and clay,
Jesus Christ was born the night before Christmas.

Come out all, come outside. You'll see something lovely.
A branch so fine-looking, all covered with flowers.

Oranges and limes, limes and oh! sweet lemons.
Prettier is the Virgin than all of the flowers.

In this Mexican tradition that began in Veracruz, Mexico, children and sometimes adults
form a procession holding a tree branch all decorated with lights, flowers, and pieces of
colored paper. They go from house to house singing and asking for their *aguinaldo*
(Christmas present). In this case, it would be candy or sometimes coins.

Pasito a pasito

Pasito a pasito
que ha nacido un sol
que a todos alumbra
con su resplandor.

VENEZUELA

Slowly, Slowly

Slowly, slowly, slowly,
The rising sun is born.
Bathing all mankind
In its gleaming light.

Brincan y bailan

Brincan y bailan
los peces en el río;
brincan y bailan
de ver al Dios nacido.

Brincan y bailan
los peces en el agua;
brincan y bailan
de ver nacida el alba.

PUERTO RICO

Leaping and Dancing

Leaping and dancing,
The fish are in the river.
Leaping and dancing,
To see the King is born.

Leaping and dancing,
The fish are in the water.
Leaping and dancing,
To see the birth of dawn.

La piñata

La piñata de esta noche
parece una estrella.
Vengan todos a gustar
y divertirse con ella.

Dale, dale, dale,
no pierdas el tino;
mide la distancia
que hay en el camino.

MEXICO

The Piñata

This evening's piñata
Looks just like a star.
Hurry over for a taste
Let's have fun with it tonight!

Hit it, hit it, hit it,
Don't lose your good aim.
Measure out the distance,
From here to there.

En México, en noches de posadas, las canciones litúrgicas culminan en el momento más esperado por los niños: la piñata! Con los ojos vendados la niña o ninõ trata de golpear fuerte la piñata hasta que se rompe, cayendo la colación (frutas, golosinas, cacahuetes y juguetitos) para gran algarabía infantil. Esta es una costumbre que también observan en El Salvador.

In Mexico, as the party escalates, the liturgic songs give way to the moment most awaited by the children; the breaking of the *piñata*. Blindfolded children try to hit it so they can get to the *colación* (mixture of candy, fruit pieces, and small toys) hidden inside. This tradition is also shared in El Salvador.

Traigo un ramillete

Traigo un ramillete,
traigo un ramillete
de un lindo rosal,
un año que viene
y otro que se va.

Vengo del olivo,
vengo del olivo,
voy pa'l olivar
un año que viene
y otro que se va.

PUERTO RICO

Bouquet of Roses

A bouquet of roses,
A bouquet of roses,
From this flowering bush;
Hark! The New Year's coming
And the old one's gone.

Olive tree, I'm leaving,
Olive tree, I'm leaving,
For the olive grove;
Hark! The New Year's coming
And the old one's gone.

Los festejos de año nuevo son tan diversos como las comunidades que los celebran, sin embargo todos tienen algo en común—el sentimiento de que un ciclo de vida termina para empezar otro. En Puerto Rico, aparte del brindis usual, se acostumbra a llenar cubos de agua para tirar a la calle a medianoche. Así se deshacen de todo lo que ha ido mal en el año pasado y dan lugar a un nuevo comienzo.

New Year's Eve celebrations are as diverse as the communities that observe them. But all have one thing in common—the feeling that one cycle of living is finished and a new one is beginning. In Puerto Rico, aside from the usual midnight toast, people assemble pails of water to throw out the window at midnight. This is to get rid of the bad and start fresh.

Los Reyes de Oriente

Los Reyes que llegaron a Belén
anunciando la llegada del Mesías
y nosotros con alegría
la anunciamos hoy también.

De tierra lejana
venimos a verte,
nos sirve de guía la
Estrella de Oriente.
¡Oh! brillante estrella
que anuncia la aurora
no me falte nunca
tu luz bienhechora.

PUERTO RICO

La epifanía es una celebración importante en America Latina envuelta
en variadas tradiciones. La Vigilia de los Reyes es una costumbre
puertorriqueña. En la víspera de Reyes, familiares y amigos se reúnen
para cantarle y rezarle a los Reyes Magos. Terminan de cantar los
misterios del rosario a la madrugada, cuando tienen una misa. Luego de
una siesta se reúnen otra vez para el banquete que incluye muchos de los
platos que se gustan en nochebuena: lechón asado, arroz con gandules,
pasteles, morcillas, alcapurrias, etc. Mientras tanto, preparándose para la
llegada de los Reyes, los niños recogen césped y lo ponen en cajas de
zapatos que esconden bajo sus camas. A la mañana siguiente, los
camellos se han comido el césped y en su lugar los Reyes Magos han
dejado juguetes para aquellos niños que aun creén.

22

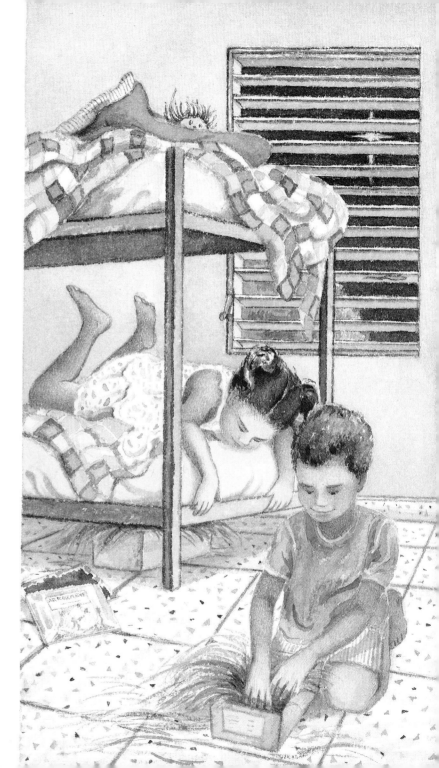

The Three Kings

The Three Kings have arrived in Bethlehem,
To announce the wonderous birth of the Messiah;
And all of us rejoicing,
Spreading word throughout the land.

From lands in the distance
We've come here to greet you.
As a guiding light,
The Eastern Star we've followed.
Oh! Great shining star!
The dawn breaks with your good news.
Please send us, we pray,
Your holy light forever.

Epiphany is a very important holiday in Latin America, surrounded by tradition. In Puerto Rico one old-time tradition is the *Vigilia de los Reyes*. Friends and family gather to sing and pray to the three kings. All the rosaries' mysteries are sung. It ends at dawn, and after mass, and sleeping a bit, there is a big feast that includes many of the foods eaten at Christmas Eve supper: roasted pig, *arroz con gandules* (rice with pigeon peas), *pasteles, morcillas* (sausages), *alcapurrias* (banana croquettes), etc. Meanwhile, in preparation for the kings' arrival, children fill shoeboxes with grass cuttings and put them under their beds. The next morning the boxes are found filled with toys. The kings came, the camels ate the grass, and just as the kings brought gifts to baby Jesus, they have brought gifts to the little children that still believe.

23

Si me dan pasteles

Si me dan pasteles,
dénmelos calientes,
que pasteles fríos,
empachan la gente.

Si me dan arroz,
no me den cuchara,
que mamá me dijo
que se lo llevara.

PUERTO RICO

If You Serve Pasteles

If you serve pasteles
Bring them steaming hot . . .
I'll end up with heartburn
If steaming hot they're not!

If you serve me rice
Don't give me a spoon
Since my mother told me
To give it all to her.

25

Las Navidades (último verso)

Con tamboriles,
güiro y maracas
mi serenata
alegre va.
Deseo a todos
por despedida
años de vida y
felicidad.

The Christmas Season (last verse)

With tambourines
Güiro and maracas
Great joy I bring with
My serenade.
Farewell, I bid you,
And God be with you,
Long life, good fortune,
And happiness.

cuatro venezolano
cuatro puertorriqueño
tamboril
güiro
pandereta
palitos
maracas

These are some of the main instruments traditionally used to accompany the Christmas songs.

He aquí algunos de los instrumentos típicos que se usan para acompañar las canciones navideñas.

Las Navidades

Por fin lle - ga - ron las Na - vi - da - des las fies - tas
Con tam - bo - ri - les, güi - ro y ma - ra - cas mi se - re -

rea - les de nues - tro lar. Fies - ta de to - dos
na - ta a - le - gre va. De - se - o a to - dos

nues - tros an - he - los, nues - tros des - ve - los, y nues - tro a - fán.
por des - pe - di - da a - ños de vi - da y fe - li - ci - dad.

The Christmas Season

It's finally here!
The Christmas season,
In regal splendor,
Has blessed our home.
This wonderous fiesta,
So deeply yearned for,
Our nights are sleepless,
With great desire.

With tambourines
Güiro and maracas
Great joy I bring with
My serenade.
Farewell, I bid you,
And God be with you,
Long life, good fortune,
And happiness.

Hermoso bouquet

Her - mo - so bou - quet — a - quí te tra - e - mos; be - llí - si - mas

flo - res del jar - dín ri - que - ño. — De to - das las flo - res —

yo te trai - go una ra - ma; — re - cí - be - lo bien que és - ta es tu a - gui - nal - do. —

Beautiful Bouquet

Beautiful bouquet
We have come to bring you
These bewitching flowers
From the lushest garden.

One of every flower
Joins this brilliant gathering
Please accept with love
My humble Christmas present.

27

Abreme la puerta

Open the Door

Open up the door, friends
In the street I'm waiting
People will start talking
Please do not ignore me.

At this very window
Roses I shall leave you
Hope they will be taken
By you, sire and lady.

Peeking through your window
See that mound so hidden —
Can it be? I hope —
A luscious suckling piglet!

Anunciación

The Annunciation

The Virgin María
Found herself with child.
And an angel told her
She was not to fear.
She will be contented
When she sees His sweet face.
From deep within her
A baby will be born.
Born will be a true God
Between mule and ox.

28

Alegría, alegría, alegría

Ha - cia Be - lén _ se en-ca-mi-na _ Ma - ría con su a - man-te es-po - so _ lle - van -

do en su _ com-pa - ñí - a _ a to-do un Dios _ po - de - ro-so. _ A - le -

grí - a a - le-grí - a a-le - grí - a; _ a - le - grí - a a - le-grí-a y pla - cer _ que la

Vir - gen _ va de pa - so _ con su es-po-so ha - cia Be - lén. _

La rama

Des - de Ve - ra - cruz _ ve - ni - mos an - dan-do y al ni - ño Je - sús _ an-da-mos bus-can-do.
En un Ja - ca - li - to de cal y de a - re - na na-ció Je - su-cris-to en la no-che bue-na.
Sal-gan pa-ra a fue-ra, ve-rán qué pri - mo-res, ve-rán a la ra-ma cu-bier-ta de flo-res.
Na-ran-jas y li - mas, li-mas y li - mo-nes:más chu-la es la Vir-gen que to-das las flo-res.

Pasito a pasito

Pa - si to a pa - si - to que ha na-ci-do un sol _

que a to - dos a - lum - bra _ con su res - plan - dor. _

Oh Rejoice, Oh Rejoice, Oh Rejoice!

To Bethlehem, they are going
Ah! María and José.
Almighty God,
    traveling with them,
He will keep them company.

Oh rejoice, Oh rejoice, Oh rejoice!
Oh rejoice, Oh rejoice, and be gay!
For approaching Bethlehem
Are María and José.

The Flowering Branch

From Veracruz we have all
    come walking,
And for Baby Jesus, we have all
    been looking.

In a little hut made
    of sand and clay,
Jesus Christ was born
    the night before Christmas.

Come out all, come outside.
    You'll see something lovely.
A branch so fine-looking,
    all covered with flowers.

Oranges and limes,
    limes and oh! sweet lemons.
Prettier is the Virgin
    than all of the flowers.

Slowly, Slowly

Slowly, slowly, slowly,
The rising sun is born.
Bathing all mankind
In its gleaming light.

29

Brincan y bailan

Leaping and Dancing

Leaping and dancing,
The fish are in the river.
Leaping and dancing,
To see the King is born.

Leaping and dancing,
The fish are in the water.
Leaping and dancing,
To see the birth of dawn.

Brin-can y bai-lan los pe-ces en el rí - o; brin-can y bai-lan de ver al Dios na-ci - do.

Brin-can y bai-lan los pe-ces en el a-gua; brin-can y bai-lan de ver na-ci-da el al-ba.

La piñata

The Piñata

Hit it, hit it, hit it,
Don't lose your good aim.
Measure out the distance,
From here to there.

Da - le, da - le, da - le, no pier-das el ti - no;

mi - de la dis - tan - cia que hay en el ca - mi - no.

Traigo un ramillete

Bouquet of Roses

A bouquet of roses,
A bouquet of roses,
From this flowering bush;
Hark! The New Year's coming
And the old one's gone.

Olive tree, I'm leaving,
Olive tree, I'm leaving,
For the olive grove;
Hark! The New Year's coming
And the old one's gone.

Trai - go un ra - mi - lle - te, trai - go un ra - mi - lle - te de un lin - do ro - sal,
Ven - go del o - li - vo, ven - go del o - li - vo, voy pa'l o - li - var,

un a - ño que vie-ne y o - tro que se va, un a - ño que vie-ne y o - tro que se va.

Los Reyes de Oriente

Los re - yes que lle - ga - ron a Be - lén, a - nun - cian - do la lle - ga - da del Me -

sí - as y no - so - tros con a - le - grí - a la a - nun - cia - mos hoy tam - bién. ¡Oh!

De tie - rra le - ja - na ve - ni - mos a ver - te, __

nos sir - ve de guí - a la Es - tre - lla de O - rien - te. __

Oh bri - llan - te es - tre - lla que a - nun - cías la au - ro - ra __

no me fal - te nun - ca tu luz bien - he - cho - ra. __

The Three Kings

The Three Kings have arrived
  in Bethlehem,
To announce the wonderous birth
  of the Messiah;
And all of us rejoicing,
Spreading word throughout
  the land.

From lands in the distance
We've come here to greet you.
As a guiding light,
The Eastern Star we've followed.
Oh! Great shining star!
The dawn breaks with
  your good news.
Please send us, we pray,
Your holy light forever.

31

Si me dan pasteles

If You Serve Pasteles

If you serve pasteles
Bring them steaming hot . . .
I'll end up with heartburn
If steaming hot they're not!

If you serve me rice
Don't give me a spoon
Since my mother told me
To give it all to her.

Si me dan pas - te - les, ___ dén - me - los ca - lien - tes, ___
Si me dan a - rroz, _____ no me den cu - cha - ra, ___

que pas - te - les frí - os, ___ em - pa - chan la gen - te. ___
que ma - má me di - jo ___ que se lo lle - va - ra. ___

Artist's Note

Christmas in Latin America is a most celebrated season, deeply swathed in rich tradition.

Unfortunately, in many countries, some of these time-cherished customs that I fondly remember from my own childhood are slowly disappearing, becoming lost to the children of the future.

In a hopeful attempt to revive some of these customs so that we can continue to share them with our children and children of other cultures, this book was created.

Beginning with December, Christmas Eve, New Years', and last, and maybe most important, Epiphany on the sixth of January, the order of the songs will help the reader travel chronologically through the season.

Las Navidades is not only a small example of the compelling and joyful Christmas songs that fill the air during the holidays, but also a glimpse of the richness and warm flavor of Latin American Christmas folklore.

So whether you've already broken a piñata or become king or queen for the day after finding the doll in the sixth of January *Rosca de Reyes* cake (recipe on the title page and page 31), find your güiro or maracas and join in the fun of these vibrant verses.(And have fun finding fourteen lizards hidden throughout the book!)

L.D.

Bibliografía/Bibliography

Navidad que vuelve, La tradición y el cantar navideño en Puerto Rico, Pedro Malavet Vega. Ponce, P.R. 1987.

La música popular de México, Jas Reuter. México: Panorama Editorial, S.A. 1981.

Del folklore musical dominicano, Julio Arzeno. Imp. la Cuna de América Roques Roman Hnos. Sto. Domingo, R.D. 1927.

Flor de villancicos, Gloria Arjona. Editorial Dpto. de Instrucción Pública, P.R. 1964.

La navidad, Christmas in Spain and Latin America, Agnes Marie Brady. National Textbook Company, 1986.

El cantar folklórico de Puerto Rico, Marcelino Canino Salgado. Editorial Universitaria, P.R. 1974.

Cantos navideños en el folklore venezolano, Isabel Aretz Thiele. Caracas Edición Casa de la Cultura Popular, 1962.

Una señora de El Salvador cuenta amorosamente del Nacimiento que solía montar para la Navidad. Hacía germinar granos de maíz, usando las plantitas como arbustos contra el fondo pintado de un paisaje salvadoreño. Su marido, quien era carpintero, le daba aserrín que ella teñía para simular lomas y caminos. Con espejos, representaba los cuerpos de agua. Usaba las diminutas figuritas de arcilla hechas por artesanos de Ilobasco, como los personajes. Con paciencia y amor recreaba todo un pueblo. Al pasar los días acercaba los Tres Reyes Magos al establo y en Nochebuena añadía el Niño Dios celebrando así su "nacimiento."